This book belongs to:

Enid Blyton's
The NEW Adventures of the Wishing~Chair

The Island of Surprises

Illustrated by Erica-Jane Waters

EGMONT

Special thanks to Narinder Dhami

EGMONT
We bring stories to life

The New Adventures of the Wishing-Chair:
The Island of Surprises
First published in Great Britain 2009
by Egmont UK Limited
239 Kensington High Street
London W8 6SA

ISBN 978 1 4052 4387 2

1 3 5 7 9 10 8 6 4 2

www.egmont.co.uk

A CIP catalogue record for this title
is available from the British Library

Printed and bound in Great Britain by Clay Ltd, St Ives plc

Contents

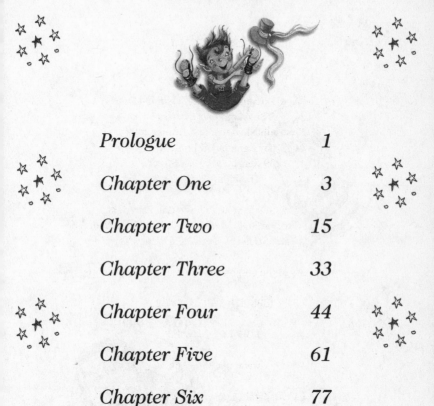

The Characters

Jack

Jessica

Flick

Toymaker

Wishler

Prologue

Wishler the pixie sighed as he stared out of the window. He had no one to talk to, and he was feeling very lonely.

Outside, he could see two children in the garden. The little pixie longed

 to go and say
hello, but he
couldn't.

'Oh, if only
I'd listened to the Toymaker,'
Wishler said sadly to himself. 'Then
I wouldn't be trapped here in this
shed, at the bottom of the garden, all
alone . . .'

Chapter
One

'I'm bored,' Jessica Campbell said, sitting down on the garden bench.

'I'm more bored than the most bored person *ever*,' her younger brother Jack replied. His face was glum as he kicked a stone across the patio floor.

'I wish we'd never come to live here.'

Jack and Jessica had just moved from the city to a village by the sea because their father had started a new job.

'It figures that this village is called Noware,' Jessica said, staring at the bottom of the long garden where a ramshackle old shed stood. 'We *are* in the middle of nowhere!'

 4

Through the dusty windows of the old shed, Jessica could just make out the shadowy shapes of various boxes. 'Why don't we go and see what's in the shed?' she suggested.

Jack shrugged. 'Sure.'

'Race you!' Jessica yelled, jumping up and running ahead.

'You're on!' Jack called back, and

they sprinted to the bottom of the garden.

Jack reached the shed first and  pulled back the rusty latch. The door creaked open. 'I don't

think anyone has been

in here for years,'

Jack said, looking at the cobwebs that

spanned the ceiling and covered the

dusty boxes and paint pots that were

piled up on the floor.

Jack went over to investigate

what was in the boxes while Jessica

examined a wooden rocking-chair,

which stood beside the window. She gasped as she noticed a patch of gold on the back of the chair. She rubbed at it with her finger, making the patch larger and larger, until a picture of a snow-white unicorn appeared, her golden horn gleaming.

'Wow!' Jessica exclaimed, as she realised that there were other painted

pictures on the chair, underneath the thick dust. 'Jack, come and look at this.'

Her brother hurried over and Jessica wiped another dusty area with her finger to reveal an emerald-green dragon.

'That's really cool!' Jack said. 'Let's clean the chair up properly, so that

we can see all the pictures.'

They found a couple of old cloths

and began wiping the chair. As Jack

rubbed at the wooden surface, he revealed a large image of an unusual looking creature. It looked like a small boy but he had long fingers and very pointy ears. He wore a bright red waistcoat, blue trousers and a jaunty green hat. Jack polished the painted figure more vigorously, so that he could have a proper look at the face.

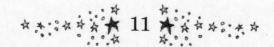

'*Atishoo*,' the image suddenly sneezed, blinking up at them. 'Stop that. It tickles!'

Jack jumped back with a gasp, as the creature peeled himself away from the chair, bit by bit.

Jack and Jessica watched in amazement as the strange boy pulled himself completely off the chair

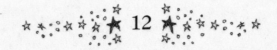

and shook off the dust. He was now

completely solid and life-like.

'Ah, that's better!' he exclaimed.

Then he beamed at Jack and Jessica.

'I'm Wishler the pixie,' he said, 'and

I'm very pleased to meet you!'

Chapter Two

'P-pixie?' Jack stammered. He glanced at Jessica whose eyes were wide open in shock.

Wishler nodded. 'I've been trapped in the chair for ages. But somehow you freed me when you dusted it.

Thank you very much.'

'You're welcome,' Jessica managed to whisper.

Wishler's cheeky little pixie face broke into a smile. 'What are your names?'

'I'm Jessica and I'm eight,' Jessica replied, smiling back. 'This is my brother, Jack, and he's seven. How old

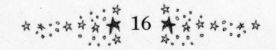

are you, Wishler?'

'Oh, I'm not quite sure,' Wishler said, crinkling up his snub nose. 'But not more than a hundred years old.'

Jack swallowed down his shock. 'How did you get trapped in the rocking-chair?'

'Well, this is a wishing-chair

actually,' Wishler replied.

'A wishing-chair?' both Jack and Jessica repeated, glancing at each other in amazement.

Wishler nodded. 'If you rock it three times and make a wish, the chair will take you to a magical land, or any time or place in the human world. I, myself, come from the Island of Surprises.'

'But how did you get here?' Jessica asked.

'I'll show you,' Wishler said. 'The wishing-chair can play back all of its adventures. You just have to ask it nicely.' He placed his hand on the arm of the chair. 'Please show us how I left the Island of Surprises!'

To Jack and Jessica's amazement, the painted pictures on the back of the chair began to swirl into each other and then started to form a new image.

'This is just like watching TV!' Jack said, as an enormous room, full of toys, came into view.

'Are these all your toys, Wishler?'

Jessica asked in disbelief.

'No, they were created by the Toymaker,' the pixie replied. 'This is his castle, and I used to work for him.'

A man with a long, white beard, wearing a blue robe, walked on to the scene. Wishler skipped along beside him. They went over to a familiar-looking chair.

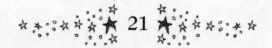

'It's the wishing-chair!' Jessica exclaimed. 'But it looks so clean and brand new.'

'It was in a bad state when the Toy-maker found it,' Wishler explained. 'The chair used to have wings but three were broken, so he built rockers for it instead.'

'Hang on,' said Jack. 'The Toy-maker's saying something!'

'You must be very careful when you polish the chair, Wishler,' the

Toymaker said, as he and the pixie picked the chair up and slowly placed it on two wooden blocks. 'The new wishing magic I've just given it will take a while to settle down and work properly. You mustn't sit on the chair just yet.'

'I won't,' Wishler promised and the wizard smiled and strolled out

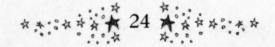

of the room.

The pixie picked up a cloth and vigorously began polishing. Soon, though, he was yawning and rubbing at his eyes tiredly and, almost as if he was half asleep already, he slumped into the chair to have a rest.

Jack and Jessica watched in dismay, as the chair fell off its blocks

and began to rock backwards and forwards.

'Stop!' Wishler shouted as he tried to scramble out of the chair. 'Please, I don't want to go anywhere. Take me nowhere!'

However, on the third rock, there was a flash of blue light and the pixie and the chair vanished.

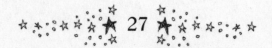 27

'I've been trapped in the chair ever since,' Wishler murmured, as the chair's normal pictures returned. 'The magic was still unstable and fused us together.'

'But how did you end up in our shed?' Jack asked frowning.

'Don't you see?' Jessica replied. 'Our village is called Noware and

Wishler said, "Take me nowhere"!'

'Oh!' Wishler gasped, his eyes opening wide. 'So *that's* why I came here.'

'But you're free now.' Jack grinned. 'You can wish to go back home to the Island of Surprises.'

Wishler shook his head sadly. 'I don't think I'm big enough to rock

the chair by myself.'

'We'll help you, Wishler,' Jessica offered.

'We'd love to see the Island of Surprises,' Jack added.

'Really?' The pixie's face lit up. 'All aboard the wishing-chair, then!'

Jack, Jessica and Wishler squeezed themselves on to the large wooden

seat and began to rock the chair

with all their might.

'*One!*' Jessica called.

'Two!' Wishler cheered.

Jack looked down and saw bright blue sparks flashing around the rockers of the wishing-chair. 'Take us to the Island of Surprises!' he shouted. *'Three!'*

Chapter
Three

Jack and Jessica tumbled out of the
wishing-chair and landed on a sandy
surface next to Wishler. They all
climbed unsteadily to their feet.

'I'm home,' Wishler declared
looking all about. 'Welcome to the

Island of Surprises!'

Jack and Jessica gazed around.

They had landed

on a beach, but

it was nothing

like the beach

back in Noware.

The sand was a

snowy white, the

sea was a vivid purple colour and the palm trees dotted here and there had bright multi-coloured leaves.

'I can see why it's called the Island of Surprises!' Jack laughed.

But Jessica didn't reply. She was staring at the wishing-chair anxiously. 'I'm not sure about this surprise,' she said. 'The chair's turned into sand!'

Jack looked at the chair in dismay.

It wasn't wooden any longer. It was

now made up of thousands of grains of the bright white sand.

'Do you think the magic will still work, Wishler?' Jack asked, touching the wishing-chair cautiously. To his horror, the sandy chair immediately crumbled under his fingers.

'Oh no!' Jessica groaned. She stared down at the pile of sand which used

to be the wishing-chair. 'How will we get home?'

'I'm sorry,' Wishler said, looking very upset. 'I didn't know that this was going to happen.'

'Let's try and rebuild it,' Jack suggested.

The three of them knelt down and tried to mould the heap of sand back

into the shape of the wishing-chair. But the grains just wouldn't stick together.

'This isn't working.' Jack rubbed a few grains of sand between his fingers. 'There's something funny about this sand.'

Wishler scooped up a handful of sand and popped it into his mouth.

Jack and Jessica stared at him in disbelief.

'Mmm, it tastes about right,' Wishler mumbled.

Bravely, Jessica licked a few grains of sand from her fingers. 'Jack, it's not sand at all!' She laughed. 'It's sugar!'

Jack took a taste too. 'Yum!'

'But what are we going to do about

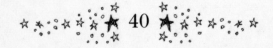

the chair?' Jessica asked. 'We have to get home before Mum finds out we're gone.'

'The Toymaker will be able to fix the chair,' Wishler told her. 'He has a repair manual for everything he's ever made. I'll take you to his castle. The quickest way is through the See-Me tunnel.'

'The See-Me tunnel?' Jack repeated.

Wishler nodded. 'I've never been

through the tunnel myself,' he said. 'But I've been told that some *very* surprising things can happen in there!'

Chapter
Four

Wishler led Jack and Jessica away from the beach and into a small, dark forest. Amazingly, as the three friends passed by, the trees held out their branches to shake hands.

They stopped in front of a large hole

in the side of a mossy bank. 'That's
the entrance to the See-Me tunnel,'
said Wishler.

The three of them climbed into
the tunnel and Jessica felt rather
nervous as darkness
surrounded them.

'Look, there's
a light up ahead!'

Jack pointed towards a strange glow that was coming from one section of the tunnel's wall.

As they got closer to the light, Jessica spotted three figures in the tunnel in front of them. It gave her a start until she realised that the walls of the tunnel were made out of mirrors, and the three figures were

their own reflections. There was one difference though – these reflections were carrying flaming torches.

'Look, it's *us*!' Jessica exclaimed, pointing at the tunnel wall.

'But *we're* not carrying torches,' Jack gasped out, staring at himself in the mirror.

'I told you surprising things can

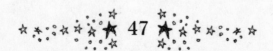

happen in this tunnel,' Wishler said with a grin.

The three reflections waved at Jack, Jessica and Wishler.

'Follow us!' called the reflected Wishler. 'We'll get you out of here.'

But Jack couldn't resist putting his face close to the mirror to take a better look at the reflections.

Suddenly, Jack's reflection reached

out of the mirror and gave his nose a

playful tug.

'Stop gawping, Jack, and get a move on!' the reflection said cheekily.

Both the reflected and the real Wishler and Jessica burst out laughing.

'Serves me right for staring!' Jack smiled as his reflection winked at him and headed off down the tunnel.

They all followed the reflections

down the tunnel. There wasn't much time for talking, though, because Jack, Jessica and Wishler had to run to keep up with their reflected selves.

Several times, the tunnel split into different paths and Jack and Jessica were very relieved that their reflections were guiding them. Otherwise, they might have been

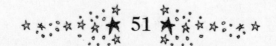

stuck in the See-Me tunnel for hours!

Eventually, their reflections came to a stop at the bottom of a long pathway.

'Here's the exit,' said the reflected Jessica, lodging her torch in a crevice in the wall. 'Good luck!'

Wishler, Jack and Jessica stared

in dismay at the tunnel exit. It was blocked with huge boulders that were piled one on top of the other. They turned round to ask their reflected selves for help but they had already gone.

'Our reflections must have brought us the wrong way,' Wishler wailed.

Jessica frowned. 'Maybe this *isn't*

the wrong way,' she said slowly. 'After all, this is the Island of Surprises and things are never quite what they seem!'

She touched one of the boulders and grinned as it squished under her fingers. 'It *looks* like a boulder, but it *feels* like a balloon!' Jessica laughed. 'I think I have an idea.'

She pulled a hairgrip from her ponytail and poked the boulder. It burst just like a balloon with a loud *pop*.

'We'll be out of here in no time,' said Jessica, handing two more hairgrips to Wishler and Jack.

The three of them began popping the squishy boulders until the exit

was clear to see.

'Brilliant idea, Jessica!' Jack said and strode out of the tunnel. Wishler grabbed his arm.

'Be careful!' the pixie warned.

Jack looked down and saw that he was standing on the edge of a deep, rocky chasm. He gulped. Wishler had stopped him just in time. On

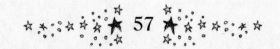

the other side of
the chasm, he
could see a castle
on a hill.

'That's the Toymaker's castle,'
Wishler explained.

'How do we get over there?' Jessica
wondered.

Jack noticed a narrow wooden

bridge across the gap and pointed it out. 'That way,' he said, setting off across the bridge.

Jessica and Wishler followed right behind. Jessica noticed that the pixie looked rather scared. She did not blame him. They were *very* high up! The bridge didn't feel very safe either, as it swayed unsteadily

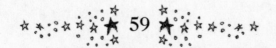

in the wind. Jessica felt dizzy.

They were halfway across the bridge when, suddenly, the wooden planks of the bridge disappeared from beneath their feet. The bridge had vanished into thin air!

With a scream, Wishler, Jack and Jessica plunged towards the rocky floor of the chasm.

Chapter
Five

Jessica squeezed her eyes shut as she fell; her heart pounded loudly in her chest.

All of a sudden, Jessica felt herself slow down, until she was hovering in mid air.

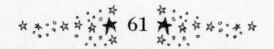

'We're flying!' Jack shouted.

Jessica opened her eyes and to her astonishment, she saw that tiny wings had sprung out of the heels of

her shoes. She looked over at Wishler
and Jack and the same thing had
happened to their shoes.

Shooting higher in the sky, Wishler,

Jessica and Jack flew across to the other side of the chasm.

'I've always wanted to fly,' Jessica said with a whoop, as the wind rushed past her ears.

A moment later, the three of them landed safely on the other side and the wings disappeared.

'Surprising things always happen

on the Island of Surprises,' Wishler said. 'But perhaps a disappearing bridge was a bit *too* surprising.'

'Yes, you were nearly turned into strawberry jam!' said a voice behind them.

Wishler, Jack and Jessica turned round and saw a young man with bright red hair and a freckly face.

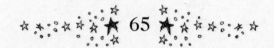

He wore an emerald green cloak and a pointy hat.

'Hello, Wishler,' the young man said.

'Flick!' Wishler exclaimed. 'Wow, you've actually got your own hat. You're a fully fledged

wizard now, I can see!'

'Well, you have been gone a long time,' Flick replied. 'Everyone wondered where you got to.'

Wishler sighed. 'The wishing-chair accidently trapped me in Jack and Jessica's shed,' he explained. 'They freed me and helped me get back, but now the chair's a pile of sugar!

I need the Toymaker's manual to fix the chair and send Jack and Jessica back home.'

'But the Toymaker is furious with you for disobeying him,' Flick said, much to Jack and Jessica's disappointment. 'I'll bet my pointy hat he won't help you!'

Wishler looked upset. 'What should

we do then?'

Flick stroked his chin. 'You could sneak into the castle and check the wishing-chair manual without the Toymaker seeing you.'

Jessica could see that Wishler didn't like this idea. 'It's not like we're going to steal the manual,' she said. 'We just want to have a quick look at it.' She laid a comforting hand on Wishler's shoulder. Strangely, just for an instant, the pixie seemed to flicker in and out of sight. Jessica blinked. Had she imagined it?

'You're right, Flick,' Wishler said. 'It's the only way.'

'Then let's go,' the wizard said. 'I'll walk with you for a little bit.'

The four of them set off towards the castle. As they followed the path through the fields, Jack noticed a golden pond shimmering in the sunshine.

'It's a honey pond,' Wishler explained.

Jack bent down, dipped his finger in the golden pool and licked it. 'Mmm,

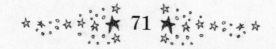

it's the best honey I've ever tasted,'

he said. 'And look at *those*!'

Jack pointed at the tall golden

reeds growing around the edge of the pond. He broke off a piece of reed and examined it. 'It's honeycomb!' He tucked it away in his pocket for later, just in case he felt a bit hungry.

'Will it be easy to sneak into the Toymaker's castle?' Jessica asked Flick, when they reached the bottom of the hill.

'Not at all,' Flick replied. 'It's guarded by a teddy-bear.'

'It can't be very hard to get past a teddy-bear,' Jack scoffed.

'This teddy-bear is as tall as the castle gates and has a mean temper,' Flick explained. 'Especially when he's hungry.'

'Maybe we can distract the teddy-

bear somehow,' Wishler suggested.

Flick shook his head. 'There's only one way to get past that teddy-bear and that's to be invisible.' Flick took a small leather pouch from his pocket. 'Luckily, I have some invisibility powder.'

'Thanks, Flick!' Wishler said in unison with Jack and Jessica.

Flick sprinkled the three of them with a sparkling green powder. Jack gazed down at himself, waiting for the magic to start working. How would it feel to be invisible?

Chapter Six

'Hey, I can still see myself,' Jack said, frowning. '*And* I can still see Wishler and Jessica!'

'You can see each other but you're invisible to everyone else,' Flick explained. 'I can't see you. I can only

hear your voices. Hurry now, the magic doesn't last very long. Good luck!'

Calling goodbye, Wishler, Jack and Jessica began to climb the hill to the castle.

When they reached the top, they could see the teddy-bear marching up and down outside the wooden door

of the castle. He looked just like an
ordinary, cuddly teddy-bear except
that he was very big indeed.

'He's cute!' Jessica said in a low voice. 'Come on, let's go inside.'

'Let's wait until the bear marches away from the door again,' Jack pointed out. 'He can't see us but he might hear us.'

They watched the bear walk past the door again.

'NOW!' Wishler said.

The three of them ran up towards the castle door, but at the same moment the bear turned and stared straight at them.

'Is he looking at us?' Jessica asked.

'Of course not, we're invisible,' Jack said confidently, reaching out to push the door open.

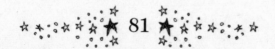

'GRRRRR!' the teddy-bear roared furiously.

'We're definitely not invisible,' Jessica yelled.

'What are we going to do?' Wishler shouted, as the bear charged towards them.

Jack remembered the honeycomb reed in his pocket. *Bears love honey,* he thought. He pulled the reed out and held it high above his head to attract the teddy-bear's attention.

Just when he was upon them, the teddy-bear skidded to a halt. He bent down and gently sniffed the honeycomb with interest. Then he held out his big, furry paw and grabbed it.

Jack backed slowly away as the teddy-bear put out his fabric tongue and gave the honeycomb reed a lick. 'Let's go!' he whispered, and the three of them dashed into the castle.

Once inside, Wishler rushed over to a golden spiral staircase. 'Follow me!' he urged. 'We must hurry.'

They ran up the steps into one of the castle's tall towers. At the top of the staircase, Wishler pushed open a heavy wooden door and they all stepped inside.

'This is the room that we saw

in pictures on the wishing-chair,'
cried Jessica, gazing round at all
the wonderful toys stacked on the
shelves.

Wishler nodded and hurried over
to a bookcase in the corner. 'This
is where the Toymaker keeps his
manuals,' he explained. 'We must find
the one for the wishing-chair!'

Jack and Jessica rushed to help
him.

'Here!' Jack said after a moment,

holding up a silver book that had

The Wishing-Chair Manual written on the front.

The three of them begin to flip through the pages.

'And what do you think you're doing?' an angry voice demanded from behind them.

Chapter
Seven

Jack and Jessica turned to see a man with a long, white beard and a blue robe glaring at them.

Jack remembered seeing him in the wishing-chair images. 'It's the Toymaker!' he whispered.

'So you're back,' the Toymaker said looking at Wishler sternly, as the pixie tried to hide the book behind his back.

'Yes, Toymaker,' the pixie said miserably. 'I'm sorry. I just wanted to look at the wishing-chair manual. I need to fix it.'

The Toymaker held out his hand

and Wishler sheepishly handed over

the manual. 'Why didn't you come and

ask me for help instead of sneaking around?'

'We're very sorry that we didn't ask your permission,' Jessica said. 'But Flick said that you were angry with Wishler and wouldn't help us.'

'Hmm,' the Toymaker said, stroking his beard. 'Flick is not a wizard to be trusted. He likes to pull all kinds of pranks.'

Jack glanced at Jessica. 'Just like invisibility powder that didn't work.'

Wishler was looking very embarrassed. 'Jack and Jessica freed me from the wishing-chair and got me back to the Island of Surprises,' he said. 'I just wanted to get them home safely.'

'You'd better tell me the whole story from the beginning,' the Toymaker said.

Wishler explained everything that had happened to him since he had been whisked away from the Island of Surprises.

'Well, you don't need my help to send Jack and Jessica home,'

the Toymaker replied, taking the manual from Wishler. 'The chair is just disguising itself. All you need to do is tap it three times, say "*Show yourself*", and the chair will go back to its normal form.'

'Really?' Jack gasped.

The Toymaker nodded. 'Then, rock it three times and say "*Home*",

and the chair will take you there.'

The Toymaker smiled at the little pixie.

'Wishler, I have missed you. Will you come back to work for me and help me invent more wonderful toys?'

'I would like that, Toymaker,'

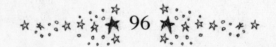

Wishler replied, his face lighting up. 'I'm so glad you're not angry with me.'

The Toymaker shook his head. 'Everyone makes mistakes.' He turned to Jack and Jessica. 'You've both been a great help to Wishler,' he said. 'Only people with very kind hearts would have been able to free

him. Being kind to other people is a type of magic in itself, you know.'

He looked from Jack to Jessica. 'As a thank you gift, I would like to give you the wishing-chair. Then you can have some wonderful adventures, but also help those who are in trouble.'

Jack and Jessica could hardly believe their ears.

'Thanks, Toymaker!' they said at
the same time.

'All you have to do is say the name of the place you wish to visit, and the chair will take you there.' The Toymaker handed them the silver manual for the wishing-chair. 'And if you have any troubles, just look at this. I'm sure you'll have lots of exciting adventures.'

'I bet we will,' Jack said happily.

Jessica didn't say anything because she was staring at Wishler. Just like before, the pixie was flickering in and out of focus, almost like he was fading away.

'Wishler, what's happening to you?' Jessica cried.

Chapter *Eight*

The Toymaker glanced at Wishler.

'Ah, I see what's going on,' he said.

'Because Wishler has been trapped in

the chair for so long, the two of them

have become linked. When Wishler

begins to flicker, it means that the

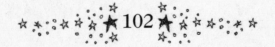

chair is impatient to leave.'

'Will I be like this forever?' Wishler stared down at his hands as they flickered in and out of focus.

The Toymaker shook his head. 'Now that you're free from the wishing-chair, the link between you will gradually begin to fade,' he explained. 'But it might take some time.'

The Toymaker turned to Jack and Jessica. 'Never leave the wishing-chair for too long or it will depart without you, and you don't want that to happen!'

Jack nodded. 'We'll take good care of the chair,' Jessica promised.

'And now it's time for you to leave.' The Toymaker snapped his fingers

and a fluffy white cloud sailed in through the open window. 'Climb on to the magic cloud and it will take you back to the wishing-chair.'

'Goodbye, Wishler,' said Jack, climbing on to the cloud as Jessica gave the pixie a hug. 'Thanks for everything!'

'I'll miss you,' Wishler said sadly.

'We'll miss you too,' Jack and Jessica said together. They hadn't known Wishler for long but he had become a very good friend.

Jessica sat on the white cloud next to Jack. It was soft and bouncy like a comfy bed. They both waved at Wishler and the Toymaker as it floated out of the window.

The cloud drifted quickly away from the castle, across the rocky chasm and then over the top of the forest where the See-Me tunnel was found.

'There's the chair,' said Jack, pointing at the large pile of sugar as the cloud came to rest on the beach.

'I hope this works,' Jessica said

nervously, climbing off the cloud. She tapped the heap of sugar three times and said, 'Show yourself!'

There was a flash of bright blue light, and suddenly the wishing-chair was back in front of them. Jack and Jessica heaved a sigh of relief as they scrambled on to the seat and began to rock.

'Home!' shouted Jack.

There was a bigger burst of blue

sparks this time and Jack and Jessica

clung on to the arms of the chair, as they were transported back to the dusty old shed.

'What an adventure!' Jack exclaimed, jumping off the wishing-chair.

'The Island of Surprises was wonderful,' said Jessica. 'But I'm glad that we're home.'

'Yes, I suppose,' Jack agreed, 'but I'm missing Wishler already.'

'Me too.' Jessica sighed.

'Ahem!' A little cough came from the corner of the room.

Jack and Jessica whirled round. To their amazement, there stood Wishler!

'What are you doing here?' Jessica said with a gasp, as she and Jack rushed over to him. 'Well, I felt *quite* sad once you'd left,' Wishler explained shyly. 'So the Toymaker very kindly said I could come back. He sent me here with one of his spells.'

'How long can you stay?' Jack asked the pixie.

Wishler beamed. 'For as long as I like!'

Jack and Jessica glanced at each other in delight.

'We're all together again!' Jessica said.

'*And* we're going to have so many more magical adventures!' Jack laughed. 'I wonder where our

wishing-chair will take us next time.'

EGMONT PRESS: ETHICAL PUBLISHING

Egmont Press is about turning writers into successful authors and children into passionate readers – producing books that enrich and entertain. As a responsible children's publisher, we go even further, considering the world in which our consumers are growing up.

Safety First
Naturally, all of our books meet legal safety requirements. But we go further than this; every book with play value is tested to the highest standards – if it fails, it's back to the drawing-board.

Made Fairly
We are working to ensure that the workers involved in our supply chain – the people that make our books – are treated with fairness and respect.

Responsible Forestry
We are committed to ensuring all our papers come from environmentally and socially responsible forest sources.

**For more information, please visit our website at
www.egmont.co.uk/ethical**